For Reginald and Hunter

'Glorious pictures and an amusing story' *Yorkshire Post*

'A treat . . . marvellous watercolour illustrations enhance the crisp telling of a very special book' *Publishers Weekly*

'Cheese addicts will have fun, and Ralph Steadman's dexterity in characterising the mice, as well as the eager brilliance of the Inspector himself, must make this a winner' *Now*

'Ralph Steadman's sophisticated underworld will provide wry humour for the adult reader too' *Mother*

Inspector MOUSE

Inspector MOUSE

by Bernard STONE and Ralph STEADman

A Sparrow Book

Published by Arrow Books 17–21 Conway Street, London W1P 6JD.
An imprint of the Hutchinson Publishing Group
London Melbourne Sydney Auckland Johannesburg
and agencies throughout the world
First published by Andersen Press 1980/Sparrow edition 1982
Reprinted 1984
Text © Bernard Stone 1980
Illustrations © Ralph Steadman 1980
All rights reserved
Printed in Italy by Grafiche AZ, Verona

ISBN 0 09 928500 2

Fatty Mouse couldn't believe his eyes. He looked around the store. All the shelves were empty. There wasn't a piece of cheese in sight. Someone had found their secret hoard and stolen it all. This was a case for Inspector Mouse.

Inspector Mouse soon arrived on the scene with his good friend Toothy Mouse. "Thank goodness you've come," wailed Fatty Mouse. "There's been a robbery! Not a morsel of cheese left. They've taken it all."

"Hmm,"said Inspector Mouse, and glanced about the store. His sharp eyes picked up a clue at once. "Pin-Stripe Mouse,"he muttered.

"How on earth can you tell?" gasped Fatty Mouse, obviously impressed.

"I thought he was on our side," said Toothy, taking out his magnifying glass.

"Never mind, Toothy. Just follow me," replied Inspector Mouse, mysteriously. *"We'll* get to the bottom of it!"

They made their way down to the Danish Blue Cheese
Club at the harbour.

The club band, "The Roquefours", were playing as they entered the club. Joe Mozzarella Mouse was the drummer. The pianist was Duke Emmental Mouse, the saxophonist was the famous Camembert Coleman Mouse and the singer was the glamorous Dolcelatte Mouse.

Inspector Mouse strolled over to the bar and turned to face Informer Mouse.

"O.K," he said. "Where's Pin-Stripe Mouse?"

Informer Mouse trembled with fear. "Sure—he's—he's down at the old fish warehouse on the waterfront. The gang has a hideout there," he stuttered.

Approaching the gang's hideout, Inspector Mouse and Toothy Mouse crept stealthily into the building.
"They are probably in the basement, Toothy," whispered Inspector Mouse. "Let's have a look through the trap-door."
"You're right," gasped Toothy. "And that's our cheese piled up in the middle. Let's surprise them."
"No, wait," warned Inspector Mouse. "They are all here— Pin-Stripe Mouse, Parmesan Cheese Mouse, Munster Mouse, Suntan Mouse, the lovely Betty Brie Mouse and Mr Big himself. We'll need help."
The gang was listening to the M.B.C. Television News broadcast. "News-flash! A consignment of Limburger cheese for the Lord Mayor's Banquet is now on its way up river, by barge, with a special escort of police mice."

Mr Big Mouse chuckled and his huge shoulders shook with glee. "That's for us," he said greedily. "It's the dream

cheese of every connoisseur. Let's pay them a surprise
visit. It's Limburger cheese for supper at the club tonight,
boys!"

Inspector Mouse turned
to Toothy and ordered,
"Quick, to the
pier. No time to lose.
We will watch and wait."

Meanwhile, the special police escort
glided silently up the river.

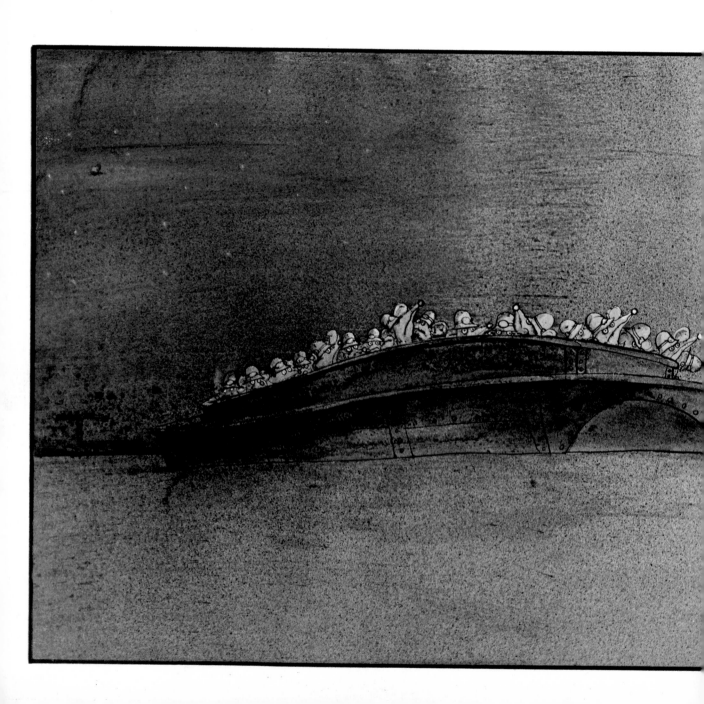

As they kept a watchful eye on the precious cargo,
the police mice began to feel very drowsy and were soon overcome
by the powerful smell of the Limburger cheese.

The gang, wearing special equipment, had no trouble at all in stealing the cheese and escaping.

Inspector Mouse watched the gang come ashore and hurry away to the club. "Don't worry, Toothy," he said. "Here come the police now, hot on their tails. Quick, into that old car. You drive."

They zoomed off
in hot pursuit,
eager for the chase.

The car spluttered to a halt
outside the Danish Blue Cheese
Club. Tumbling out of the car,
they crashed through the door
and into the Club.
"Stay where you are. This is a
raid!" shouted Inspector Mouse.
He nodded towards Pin-Stripe
Mouse who opened the drum.
There it was! The stolen cheese
from the barge.
"Oh no!" cried Joe Mozzarella
Mouse. "We've been tricked!"
Toothy was amazed. "So you
were on our side after all," he
said to Pin-Stripe Mouse.
"Elementary, my dear Toothy.
You're right as usual," said
Inspector Mouse. "I don't know
what I'd do without you.
Now why don't you play the
piano. What was that song...?"

"Play it again, Toothy."

Other books in the Sparrow/Andersen Press picture book series:

EMERGENCY MOUSE   Bernard Stone and Ralph Steadman
CRAZY CHARLIE   Ruth Brown
IF AT FIRST YOU DO NOT SEE   Ruth Brown
IF MICE COULD FLY   John Cameron
THE TIGER WHO LOST HIS STRIPES   Michael Foreman and Anthony Paul
NOT NOW BERNARD   David McKee
THE ADVENTURES OF KING ROLLO   David McKee
FURTHER ADVENTURES OF KING ROLLO   David McKee
KING ROLLO AND THE PLAYROOM   David McKee
TUSK TUSK   David McKee
THE HUNTER AND THE ANIMALS   Tomie de Paola
PUSS IN BOOTS   Tony Ross
GOLDILOCKS AND THE THREE BEARS   Tony Ross
THE THREE PIGS   Tony Ross
FEARSOME FRITZ   Jean Willis and Margaret Chamberlain